DEDICATION

To my children: Bree, Ally, Macy, and Grant. Thank you for being my constant source of inspiration and joy. Your love and support have carried me through every chapter of this journey.

To my mama, Murl. Your faith and guidance introduced me to my Lord and Savior Jesus Christ, and for that eternal gift I am forever grateful.

CONTENTS

ACKNOWLEDGMENTS

To my firstborn, Bree. Your insights, wisdom, and gentle encouragement have been a guiding light throughout this journey. Thank you for believing in your mama and reminding me to follow the dream God placed in my heart. This book carries pieces of your love and support on every page.

CHAPTER ONE: STORIES IN HER WHEELS

The house felt heavy with quiet.

Not the peaceful kind, like Sunday mornings with coffee and an empty to-do list. This was the hollow kind, the kind that echoed off the walls and made her want to crawl back into bed. Even the hum of the refrigerator seemed louder, filling the silence with a low, lonely drone.

Her youngest had left for college a week ago. The goodbye had been sweet and tearful, full of promises. But now the silence pressed harder than the memories.

She stood in the kitchen, staring at the Crock Pot she had used to feed a family for more than twenty years. Its lid was slightly chipped; the metal edges dulled from years of use. It looked tired. Or maybe she did.

Louella's phone chimed, sharp and bright against the stillness, and she raced to it with a smile. "It must be one of the kids," she thought. But her smile quickly faded. It was a listing for a vintage camper named Tess. Teal and cream, slightly dented, and parked two towns over. The photo showed sunlight glinting off its worn paint, shadows stretching across the gravel beneath it. The ad read: *She's got stories in her wheels and room for one more adventure.*

A spark of boldness rose up inside her. "You know what," she thought, "that describes me perfectly." Not wanting to give self-doubt a chance, she made the call.

Two hours later, she was standing in a gravel driveway, staring at Tess. The air smelled faintly of motor oil and pine needles. The camper was charming in a "bless her heart" kind of way. Rusted in places, but proud. Like a Southern aunt who still wore her best red lipstick to the local grocery store.

"I'll take her," she said, cutting off the seller before he could finish his pitch. The truth was, the hardest person to convince had been herself, and deep down she had already made the decision.

That night, she packed a duffel bag with jeans, a journal, and a half-used bottle of dry shampoo. She didn't know where she was going.

She just knew she couldn't stay still.

Louella video-called her kids, her voice steady but full of excitement. "I'm taking a solo road trip," she announced. The reaction was immediate. Her children stared back wide-eyed, voices overlapping with worry. "Mom, are you serious? Alone? What if something happens?" one asked. Another shook her head. "You've lost your mind. This is crazy." Their fear for her safety was real, and Louella knew it came from love.

Then four familiar faces appeared in the frame. Her oldest grandchild, a teenager, loved the idea. The two younger ones bounced with curiosity, peppering her with questions about where she was going. And the baby, perched on a hip, giggled into the camera, oblivious to the fuss.

Louella's eyes softened. "I will miss you all so much," she told them. "I will send pictures from every stop so you can see what I see. And when I get back, I will have stories to share with each of you."

Her children still looked uneasy, but the grandkids' laughter lightened the moment. Louella felt the weight of their concern, yet underneath it all was the reminder that her journey was not just for herself. It was also for them, to show that faith and courage can carry you into new chapters even when the world thinks you are a little crazy.

Louella had spent the night tossing and turning, unable to sleep. After climbing behind the wheel, she whispered a prayer. She asked God to protect her and guide her toward meaning and purpose again. She didn't know what the answer would look like, but she trusted He would show her in His time.

The sun was just rising over the Tallahassee trees. The air was cool and smelled faintly of magnolia blossoms. Spanish moss swayed like lace in the breeze. She rolled down the window, felt the cool morning air on her skin, and whispered to no one in particular:

"Let's see what's out there."

CHAPTER TWO: THE FIRST STOP

Louella hadn't driven more than thirty miles before she realized two things.

One: Tess rattled like a tambourine on wheels.

Two: She hadn't packed any coffee.

The Florida sun was climbing fast, casting long shadows across the two-lane highway. The camper's tiny fan whirred like it was trying to keep up, and the scent of warm vinyl and old upholstery filled the air. She cracked the window, letting in a breeze that smelled faintly of farmland and pavement.

As she crossed into Holmes County, memories stirred. This was where she had grown up, raised her family, and watched her roots sink deep into red clay roads and small-town life. Sundays with her mama at the little white church came rushing back—potluck dinners, hymns sung full of heart, and neighbors who were family in every way that mattered. The majority of her family still lived there, keeping the ties strong and the memories alive.

She remembered countless nights in that same country church, her mama and two best friends standing with hands lifted high, crying out to God until they prayed through. The Spirit of the Lord would fill that little wooden sanctuary so completely that you could feel His presence pressing against your body, commanding reverence for His house. Even as a child she knew deep within her that God was real and alive, because what she experienced was not hyped-up emotionalism. It was a quiet, undeniable force that could not be dismissed.

Her mother had taught her the power of godly friendships, nights spent in prayer with women who never sought recognition but whose faith moved mountains. And as the oldest of six siblings, Louella had learned early how to carry responsibility, how to listen, and how to lean on God when the noise of life pressed in. Holmes County was not just a place on the map. It was the soil where God had planted her roots, shaping her through family, friendships, and faith. The prayers of her mama and those faithful women had moved heaven, not because of their power, but because of God's.

Lost in thought as the miles rolled by, she eventually rounded a bend and spotted a roadside diner. The sign read *Dot's Place* in faded red letters, with a hand-painted coffee cup underneath. The parking lot was gravel, the kind that crunched under tires and crept into sandals.

The diner's air smelled of bacon grease mixed with lemon cleaner. When she picked up the laminated menu, her fingers caught the tacky chill of leftover grape jelly. A silver-haired waitress named Darla approached with a smile. "Coffee and a biscuit?" Darla asked, already pouring.

Louella nodded. "And maybe a little hope, if you've got it."

Darla winked. "Honey, we serve that fresh every morning."

Louella sat by the window, watching Tess through the glass. The camper looked small and brave, parked between a pickup truck and a rusty sedan. She pulled out her journal and wrote:

Biscuit was flaky. Coffee was strong. I didn't cry when I left. That feels like progress.

Without so much as a pause for permission, a woman slid into the booth across from Louella. She was dressed in a lavender pantsuit and white sneakers, her layers of costume jewelry catching the light like a disco ball. The bangles on her wrist clinked cheerfully as she set down her coffee.

Louella blinked, startled but not entirely surprised. Her life had always been dotted with these impromptu encounters, strangers who seemed compelled to spill their stories the moment they met her. She often joked that she'd missed her calling as a bartender, the kind of listener people instinctively trusted with their secrets.

"You're the one with the camper," the woman said, her voice warm and raspy. "I saw you pull in. That teal beauty caught my eye."

Louella smiled. "Yes, ma'am. Just started out this morning."

The woman grinned, revealing lipstick slightly outside the lines and a confidence that didn't care. "Name's Birdie. I've been on the road since '92. Lost my Harold years back. Since then, the camper's been my home and my companion."

Louella laughed softly. "I'm not sure I know what I'm doing."

Birdie leaned in, her rings tapping the table. "Darlin', if you waited until you were sure, you'd never leave the driveway. You're doing just fine."

Louella hesitated, then lowered her voice. "Before I left, I said a prayer. I asked God to protect me and help me find my meaning and purpose again. I don't know what that looks like yet, but I'm hoping this trip is part of the answer."

Birdie's eyes softened. "Well, honey, you just keep that prayer close. The road has a way of answering in pieces, not all at once."

She reached into her purse and pulled out a small brooch shaped like a sunflower. "Here. For your dashboard. A little sparkle to remind you you're blooming, even if it feels messy."

Louella took it, eyes misty. "Thank you."

Birdie sipped her coffee, then added, "After years of traveling I've found myself part of a little festival community. Each year I hit up my favorites and try out a couple of new ones. I'm headed to the Magnolia Moon Festival now. It's been a regular of mine for years. Starts tomorrow. Music, pie contests, and more rhinestones than sense. Here's a flyer. You should come."

Louella hesitated. She hadn't planned anything beyond today. But the idea of music and pie and strangers who might feel like friends tugged at something deep inside her.

She smiled. "You know what? I might just do that."

Birdie grinned. "Good. I'll save you a seat at the pie judging. Hope you like blueberry."

Louella finished her breakfast and climbed into Tess, excited to have a destination.

CHAPTER THREE: A SLICE OF BELONGING

The festival smelled like corndogs, sunscreen, and fresh-cut grass. American flags proudly waved from every lamppost, and the coastal Florida town square was alive with music, laughter, and the clink of mason jars filled with sweet tea.

Louella wandered past booths selling homemade soap, embroidered aprons, and jars of pickled okra. Children darted between hay bales, their faces sticky with cotton candy.

Near the lemonade stand, she noticed a young mother juggling a baby on her hip while a toddler tugged at her skirt, whining for another balloon. The woman's face was flushed, her hair escaping its ponytail, and her eyes carried that familiar mix of exhaustion and guilt.

Louella stepped closer, her voice gentle. "You're doing just fine, dear. I remember those days. Felt like I was drowning in diapers and snack cups."

The mother sighed, shifting the baby. "My husband died in a car accident last year. And now it's just me. I don't know if I can keep doing everything alone. I wasn't built to be mom and dad. I love my kids, but I never take time for myself. There's no room for self-care when you're holding everything together."

Louella reached out to adjust the toddler's crooked balloon string, her eyes kind. "I hear you. And I'll tell you something I wish someone had told me back then. You can't pour from an empty cup. God gives us rest so we can give love. Self-care isn't selfish. It's survival, and it's holy."

The woman's eyes softened, tears threatening. "But it feels like I'm failing if I step back."

Louella shook her head. "Every person who shoulders responsibility needs rest, joy, and time to breathe. And here's another truth: children learn by watching us. If we don't handle stress and emotions in healthy ways, how can we expect them to do something we can't? It's our duty as adults to teach them how to live, not just demand they figure it out. If being a good parent or role model were easy, everyone would be one. But it's hard work, and that's why it matters."

The young mother smiled, appearing a little lighter now. "Thank you. I needed that."

Louella winked. "Now go get yourself a slice of pie. Sugar fixes more than you'd think."

Birdie was already holding court near the pie contest tent, her earrings flashing like disco lights as she told a story about a runaway goat and a Baptist wedding. Louella couldn't help but laugh. Birdie had the kind of presence that made strangers lean in just to catch the punchline.

"Darlin', you're just in time," Birdie said, waving Louella over. "They need another judge. And trust me, you don't want to miss Patty Jo's coconut cream. It's been known to cause family feuds."

Louella hesitated. "I've never judged a pie contest before."

Birdie grinned. "Well, hon, you've raised kids. You've broken up fights over juice boxes and who gets the last chicken nugget. You're more qualified than half the folks here."

The first pie arrived: pecan, glossy and rich. Louella took a bite. The sweetness hit like a hymn sung with too much gusto. "Mercy," she said, fanning herself. "That'll put you straight into a sugar coma."

Next came a blueberry pie so purple it looked like it had been dyed at Easter. Birdie leaned over. "If your tongue doesn't turn blue, they didn't put in enough berries."

By the third pie, a lopsided apple with a crust that looked like it had been patched together with duct tape, Louella was giggling. "Bless their heart," she whispered. "This one tastes like regret and cinnamon."

The crowd roared with laughter when Birdie announced, "We've got ourselves a tie between Patty Jo's coconut cream and Reverend Miller's bourbon pecan. Looks like the coconut and liquor are neck and neck."

Louella raised her fork. "Well, I say let's call it a draw. Coconut cream for Sunday, bourbon pecan for Saturday night."

The tent erupted in applause. Birdie slapped the table, her rings clinking like applause of their own. "See? You're a natural. Motherhood gave you the wisdom, but humor makes it sweet."

As the crowd laughed and bonded over pie, Louella felt joy rise in her heart. She realized God was reminding her that true belonging is not found in escape, but in the people and places He uses to show us who we are.

Journal Entry

Tonight reminded me why I cherish small-town festivals. The smell of corndogs, the laughter of children, and neighbors becoming family over pie. It felt like home. I saw myself in that young mother, weary yet determined, and pray she knows she is not alone. Birdie's humor, the crowd's joy, even the lopsided apple pie all stitched together into something bigger than me.

CHAPTER FOUR: GRACE IN THE THUNDER

By the time Louella had settled in bed, the thunder rolled. Low at first, then sharp enough to rattle the camper's thin windows. Lightning flashed, painting the inside of Tess in quick bursts of white.

Louella pulled the blanket tighter around her shoulders. She remembered nights like this when her children were small. Storms that shook the house, sending little feet running down the hallway. She would gather them in her arms, whispering stories about brave princesses or silly raccoons, even when her own heart was pounding. She had been scared too, but she never let them see it.

She smiled at the memory, realizing she had modeled calm for her children just like she had spoken to the young mother earlier that day. But she hadn't always. It had taken time, and more than a few mistakes, to understand that she couldn't get angry at her children for being children. When she felt frustration rising, it was never really about them. It was her own cup running dry, her own exhaustion spilling over.

Her children hadn't come with an instruction manual. Like them, she was learning life for the first time. She had to lean on God's grace, to accept that mistakes were part of the process. And in receiving His grace, she was able to show her children how to forgive themselves too.

Storms weren't only in the sky; they had lived in her work as well. She reached for her laptop, its glow cutting through the dark. Her retirement pension covered the bills, steady as clockwork. When she wanted extra income, she picked up consulting contracts—remote work that let her use her experience without tying her down. She hadn't built her career alone. Piece by piece, the Lord had opened doors, sustained her without a college degree, and given her perseverance and the kind of wisdom only He can teach through living.

Scrolling through old emails from clients, she thought about the good and the bad. The times she had doubted herself, the times she had triumphed. The long nights, the laughter, the heartbreaks.

And for the first time, she let herself say it out loud. "God carried me through."

The words hung in the air, steady as the thunder outside.

The storm raged on, but Louella felt calm. She wasn't just surviving. She was living in God's story, one mile, one memory, one storm at a time.

CHAPTER FIVE: MERCIES IN THE MORNING

The storm had passed by dawn, leaving the campground washed clean. Drops of rain clung to the pine needles, glittering in the early light. Louella stepped outside Tess with her *World's Best YaYa* mug, steam rising from the coffee she had brewed on the tiny stove.

She settled into a folding chair, the ground still damp beneath her flip-flops and breathed in the smell of wet earth mixed with strong coffee. For the first time in a long while, she felt rested.

An older man ambled past with a fishing pole slung over his shoulder. He tipped his cap. "Morning. You survived the storm?"

Louella smiled. "Survived and thrived. Coffee helps."

He chuckled. "There's a little lake down the road. Folks say the sunrise hits it just right. Worth the walk if you've got the time."

Louella sipped her coffee, considering. She had nowhere she had to be, no deadlines except the ones she chose. For once, her life wasn't about schedules. It was about choices.

She thought about the years she had spent raising her children, working hard, doubting herself, and pressing forward. She had often brushed off her own accomplishments, chalking them up to luck or necessity. But sitting there in the morning light, she realized she hadn't done it alone. God had carried her, helping her build something steady and good.

Birdie appeared from her camper, jangling with jewelry even at sunrise. "Well, look at you, Miss Sunshine. Ready for another adventure?"

Louella laughed. "Maybe I'll start with that lake. Seems like a good place to see what comes next."

She followed the gravel path down to the lake, the air cool and fresh after the storm. The water shimmered with streaks of gold as the sun climbed higher. Birds called across the shoreline, and the gentle lap of water against the dock made the morning feel alive. A small bait and tackle shop sat near the dock, its porch lined with buckets, nets, and faded rocking chairs.

Inside, a young man in his twenties was restocking shelves with jars of minnows and spools of fishing line. He looked up, startled, then smiled politely. "Morning, ma'am. Need anything for fishing?"

Louella shook her head. "Just walking. Thought I'd see the lake."

He nodded, then sighed, setting down the spool in his hand. "Guess you picked a good morning. I'm just trying to keep myself busy. My girlfriend thinks I was flirting with someone at the festival yesterday. Whole thing was a misunderstanding, but she won't hear it."

Louella leaned against the counter, her mug still warm in her hand. "Misunderstandings can feel bigger than they are. When my kids were teenagers, they'd swear I didn't understand them. Half the time, it was just that I hadn't listened long enough before answering."

The young man frowned. "So, you think I should just listen?"

Louella smiled. "Start there. Let her talk it out. Don't rush to defend yourself. Sometimes people just want to feel heard before they can believe the truth. And if she's worth it, you'll be patient enough to let her untangle her feelings."

He nodded slowly, relief softening his face. "I guess I've been too quick to argue. Maybe I'll try that."

Louella patted the counter. "You'll figure it out. Relationships are like fishing. You can't yank the line too hard, or you'll lose the catch. Gentle works better."

The young man chuckled. "Thanks, ma'am. That actually makes sense."

Louella stepped back onto the porch, the lake stretching wide and calm before her. She lingered for a moment, breathing in the cool air, then turned toward the gravel path. The walk back to Tess felt lighter, each step carrying a quiet peace. Inside the camper, she set her mug on the counter and settled into the familiar hum of her little home on wheels. The stillness wrapped around her, inviting reflection.

Journal Entry

The storm is gone, but its memory lingers in the drops clinging to the pine needles. This morning reminded me that God clears the skies after the fiercest nights, not just in weather but in life. As I sat with my coffee, I felt His presence in the stillness, whispering that rest is holy and renewal is possible. The lake shimmered like a promise, reminding me that His mercies are new every morning and always enough to carry me through whatever comes next. I don't have to know the whole path. I only have to trust the One who guides it.

CHAPTER SIX: BEIGNETS AND BRASS

Louella eased Tess back onto the highway, the tires humming a steady rhythm as the miles rolled beneath her. The storm was behind her now, and ahead lay New Orleans. She had a craving she couldn't shake, one that tasted of powdered sugar and brass music. Beignets and Jackson Square were calling her name.

By the time she reached the city, the air was thick with spice and rhythm. Louella parked near the French Quarter and followed her nose to a small café. The scent of garlic and cayenne drifted out the door, and soon a steaming plate of crawfish étouffée was set before her. She closed her eyes at the first bite, the flavors bold and unapologetic. It was food that sang; food that reminded her of resilience and joy.

She lingered only a moment, then stepped back into the streets, drawn toward Jackson Square where the city's heartbeat pulsed in brass horns, painted canvases, and laughter spilling across the cobblestones.

The square was alive with street performers, artists, and musicians. Brass horns blared from a corner, their notes tumbling into the air like laughter. Painters lined the iron fences, their canvases splashed with color. Tarot readers leaned over velvet tables, shuffling cards with practiced hands.

Louella paused, taking it all in. The cathedral's spires rose against the sky, white and sharp, while the square itself buzzed with energy. She felt the rhythm of the place seep into her bones. It was messy and beautiful, loud and soulful, and she loved every bit of it.

Near the cathedral steps, an older painter in a straw hat was arranging canvases. His work was vibrant, filled with swirling colors that seemed to dance off the surface. Louella stopped to admire one of a riverboat glowing under a moonlit sky.

"You like it?" the painter asked, his voice gravelly but kind.

Louella nodded. "It feels alive. Like the river's moving even though it's paint."

He smiled. "That's the trick. Paint what you feel. Not just what you see."

Louella thought about her own journey. "I've been writing lately. Trying to capture what it feels like to start over."

The painter leaned closer. "Then don't worry about perfect. Honest matters more. People don't remember the straight lines. They remember the colors that made them feel something."

His words sank deep. For years Louella had questioned her worth and overlooked the victories God had given her. But in the square, with brass horns blaring, footsteps echoing on cobblestones, and laughter spilling from every corner, she understood her story did not need polish. It needed honesty. God's grace was already painting beauty across the broken places.

She bought a small canvas of a sunrise over the Mississippi and tucked it under her arm. The city's rhythm clung to her, alive and intimate, like a heartbeat she could carry.

Louella walked back through the lively streets, music still ringing in her ears. By the time she reached Tess, the rhythm lingered in her chest. She placed the painting inside, brewed a small cup of coffee, and settled into the quiet hum of the camper. Outside, New Orleans pulsed with brass and color; inside, God gave her stillness and space to reflect.

Journal Entry

New Orleans was alive in every way; loud, messy, beautiful, and unashamed. The music and art reminded me that life does not have to be polished to be meaningful. God paints with bold colors, not straight lines, and He calls me to do the same with my story. Today I realized that honesty matters more than perfection. My journey is not about proving myself. It is about trusting Him to make beauty out of the broken places.

CHAPTER SEVEN: STRENGTH IN THE BREAKDOWN

After a few days of savoring beignets, brass music, and the wild heartbeat of New Orleans, Louella pointed Tess west. Big Bend National Park had been tugging at her imagination, a place of wide skies and rugged beauty. She wanted to see the desert stretch out in silence, to feel small in the best kind of way.

The road was long, the sun relentless. By midafternoon, the camper's engine began to whine. A thin curl of steam rose from under the hood, and the temperature gauge climbed higher than Louella had ever seen.

She pulled over to the shoulder, heart pounding. The highway stretched empty in both directions, no towns in sight. She reached for her phone, but the screen showed no signal.

Her hands trembled as she whispered a prayer. "Lord, I have made it this far. Please do not let me break down in the middle of nowhere."

The heat wrapped around her, suffocating and merciless. Her chest constricted, breath shallow and uneven. Panic surged, unstoppable, like waves crashing against a fragile shore. *What was I thinking?* she berated herself. *I am too old for this. Foolish to wander alone. Foolish to trust this forgotten road.*

She pressed her palms against the steering wheel, fighting the swirl of doubt. Her vision blurred with tears. For a moment, she felt like turning back, abandoning the road and the dream that had carried her this far.

And then, in the quiet of her fear, another thought came. It is easy to trust God when everything is smooth and certain. But faith is not built in the easy days. It is forged in the hard ones, when the road feels empty and the answers do not come right away. Louella breathed deeply, reminding herself that this moment, frightening as it was, might be part of the very lesson she had prayed for.

After what felt like hours, a dusty pickup slowed beside her. An older couple leaned out the window, faces lined with kindness.

"You look like you could use a hand," the man said.

16

Louella exhaled, relief washing over her. "The camper is overheated, no signal on my phone. And honestly, I am starting to wonder if I made a mistake. I set out to rediscover myself and trust God to lead me."

The woman shook her head gently. "Honey, do not let fear tell you lies. Rediscovering yourself is not foolish. It is brave."

The man added, "We have been married fifty years. We have had our share of breakdowns on the road and in life. The trick is not to panic. Just take the next step."

The woman leaned closer. "The desert will test you. But remember, God never leaves you alone."

Louella managed a shaky laugh. "I was starting to think I would be sleeping on the side of the road."

The man smiled. "Not today. Out here, folks look out for each other. And God looks out for you too."

The woman squeezed her hand. "Engines can be fixed. But sometimes life breaks down so God can show you the strength He has already placed within you."

Louella had been afraid, but she was not alone. God's kindness had reached her through strangers, reminding her that the road ahead was still hers to walk, and that He would walk it with her.

Journal Entry

Today the desert pushed me to my limits. The engine failed, the road stretched empty, and fear pressed hard against my chest. For a moment I believed the lies that said I was too old, too foolish, too alone. Yet in the stillness of panic, God reminded me that faith is not born in comfort. It grows in the heat, in the waiting, in the places where answers come slowly. Strangers stopped to help, and I saw His kindness reflected in their faces. Engines can be repaired, but the soul is strengthened in the breakdowns. I am not alone, and I am not defeated. The road ahead is mine to walk, and He will walk it with me.

CHAPTER EIGHT: MAIN STREET MIRRORS

With Tess in the shop for repairs, Louella checked into the only hotel in town, a squat brick building with lace curtains in the windows and a neon sign that buzzed faintly at night. The room was simple but clean, and for once she welcomed the stillness.

The next morning, she walked down to the diner on Main Street. The bell above the door jingled as she stepped inside, greeted by the smell of bacon and biscuits. Locals filled the booths, their conversations humming like background music. Louella ordered scrambled eggs, grits, and coffee, savoring the comfort of a hot breakfast she had not cooked herself.

Afterward, she strolled through town, pausing at the mom and pop shops. A hardware store with faded paint, a bakery with hand-lettered signs, and a bookstore that smelled of paper and dust. Each storefront felt like a piece of history, stitched together by the people who kept them alive.

She ducked into a thrift store, drawn by a rack of vintage scarves fluttering near the door. Inside, the air smelled faintly of lavender and old leather. As she sifted through a row of jackets, another woman about her age struck up a conversation.

"Funny thing about thrift stores," the woman said. "They remind me how much my body has changed. I used to be able to wear anything. Now I am just trying to find something that makes me feel like myself again."

Louella nodded, her voice gentle. "I know what you mean. Life changes us. But God has shown me our worth is not in smooth skin or shiny hair. It is in the stories we carry and the resilience He builds in us. Men may get called distinguished, but women like us, we are seasoned. We have lived through storms, and by His grace, we are still standing."

The woman's eyes softened. "Seasoned. I like that. Makes me feel less invisible."

Just then, a younger woman browsing the shoe rack joined in, her voice quiet but steady. "I wish my mama had heard that. She never believed she was enough."

Louella and the older woman turned toward her. She took a breath and continued. "My dad ridiculed her, said she was old and washed up. Then he left us for a younger woman. Mama sank into despair. She tried to fill the emptiness with drinking and partying. One night she overdosed."

The thrift store seemed to fall silent around them.

"My grandparents raised me," she said, eyes steady. "They saved me. And now I have two little boys of my own. I am doing everything I can to raise them to respect women, to see that beauty is more than appearances. My husband is a good man. He understands how important it is to teach our boys how women should be treated."

Louella reached out, her voice warm. "You are breaking the cycle. That is the bravest thing a woman can do. And God will honor that."

The older woman nodded. "You are showing those boys that strength and kindness matter more than looks. That is real beauty."

The young woman smiled, tears glistening but unfallen. "I just want them to grow up knowing women are not disposable. We are worth respect, no matter our age or our scars."

Louella squeezed her hand. "Because of you, they will. God is using your story to plant seeds of respect and love in their hearts."

As Louella left the shop, a scarf tucked under her arm, the conversation settled deep in her chest. The thrift store had given her more than a bargain. It had reminded her that women of every age carry battles unseen, and that God places us in each other's paths so healing can begin.

Journal Entry

Today reminded me that every woman carries battles the world may never see. In the thrift store, I heard stories of loss, resilience, and the quiet courage it takes to keep showing up. God does not measure us by smooth skin or youthful strength. He sees the scars, the seasons, and the faith that grows in the cracks. Beauty fades, but His truth endures. I believe He places us in each other's paths so we can speak life where despair has taken root. Healing begins when we share our stories, and today I saw His light shining through broken places, turning them into testimonies of hope.

Me, Again

CHAPTER NINE: HORIZON OF GRACE

The morning sun spilled across the motel curtains, painting the room in soft gold. Louella stretched, feeling the weight of yesterday's conversations still lingering in her chest. The thrift store woman's words about aging and the young mother's story of resilience had settled into her like seeds waiting to bloom.

Tess was repaired and waiting. Louella loaded her bag, tucked Birdie's sunflower brooch back onto the dashboard, and whispered a quiet prayer before turning the key. "Lord, thank You for carrying me this far. Help me keep trusting You, even when the road feels uncertain."

The highway stretched wide and empty, leading her toward Big Bend National Park. The desert air was different from Florida's humidity, dry, sharp, and vast. As miles rolled beneath her tires, she thought about how faith was easier when life was smooth. But the breakdown, the panic, the silence of no phone signal had been the real lessons. Faith is not built in comfort. It is built in the hard places, when doubt presses in and the only choice is to keep moving forward.

By late afternoon, she found a campsite tucked against a ridge. The desert spread out in every direction, painted in shades of rust and gold. As the sun dipped low, Louella built a small fire, its crackle the only sound in the vast stillness.

She was not alone for long. An older couple wandered over from the next site, both carrying a tin mug and a kind smile. "Mind if we sit a spell?" the man asked.

Louella nodded, grateful for company.

They talked easily, the way strangers sometimes do when the night invites honesty. He told her he and his wife had been traveling since retirement, chasing sunsets and quiet places. "Out here," he said, gesturing to the horizon, "you realize how small you are. But small does not mean unimportant. It means you are part of something bigger."

Louella stared into the fire. "I have been trying to rediscover myself.

Some days I feel steady. Other days, I wonder if I was foolish to even try."

The man smiled. "That is the beauty of walking with God. He does not ask us to have all the answers. He asks us to trust Him with the steps. Purpose is not something we invent. It is something we uncover as we walk. The desert does not demand perfection. It reminds you to keep moving, one step at a time."

The wife leaned forward, her eyes glistening in the firelight. "I know what it feels like to want to give up. Years ago, we lost a child. I thought my heart would never heal. I remember sitting in the dark, telling God I could not go on. But in that moment, He met me. Not with answers, but with peace. He gave me strength to take the next breath and the next step. That is when I learned faith is not about pretending the pain is not real. It is about trusting Him to carry you when you cannot carry yourself."

Her words sank deep into Louella's heart. She realized that with God there is always hope. Hope is not fragile or fleeting. It is anchored in His presence. And when we walk away from God, we also walk away from hope. That truth became the heartbeat of the night, steady and undeniable.

Later, when the stars spilled across the sky in a glittering sweep, Louella lay back and let the silence wash over her. The vastness did not scare her anymore. It steadied her. She whispered into the night, "Faith is not the absence of fear. It is the courage to keep going, trusting God to guide the way. And as long as I walk with Him, I will never be without hope."

Journal Entry

The desert stretched wide today. The couple by the fire reminded me that small does not mean insignificant. Out here, the horizon teaches humility and hope. Their story of loss pierced me, yet it carried a truth I cannot ignore. Faith is not about pretending pain does not exist. It is about trusting God to carry us when we cannot carry ourselves. Tonight, under the stars, I felt His presence steady me. Hope is not fragile. It is anchored in Him, and as long as I walk with God, I will never be without it.

Me, Again

CHAPTER TEN: WHISPERS IN THE CANYON

The next morning, Louella set out to explore Big Bend National Park. The desert stretched endlessly, its rugged cliffs rising like ancient cathedrals carved by time. The Rio Grande shimmered in the distance, winding its way through canyons that seemed to sing of eternity.

She hiked along a trail that led to a high overlook. The air was crisp, the silence profound, broken only by the call of a hawk circling above. Standing there, surrounded by the vastness of God's creation, Louella felt her breath catch. The beauty was overwhelming, too grand for words.

Her eyes filled with tears. "Lord," she whispered, "I do not always understand. I doubt. I wonder if I am strong enough, if I have made mistakes I cannot undo. I want to trust You, but sometimes the fear feels louder than faith."

The wind stirred, brushing against her face like a gentle hand. In the quiet, she felt a voice rise within her spirit, steady and tender. "My love for you is unconditional. These trials are temporary, not forever. They have a purpose, shaping you, strengthening you, drawing you closer to Me."

Louella stood still, letting the words settle deep. She realized that doubt was not unusual. Many of the greatest figures in Scripture wrestled with it. Abraham questioned God's promises. Moses wondered if he was capable of leading. David cried out in despair. Thomas struggled to believe until he saw with his own eyes. Their stories reminded her that faith is not certainty. Faith is trust. It is choosing to keep her focus on God instead of the problem.

She whispered again, "You already know my heart, Lord. You do not get angry when I confess my weakness. You do not hold it against me. You invite honesty because You are not like people who judge or compete. You are love itself."

Her thoughts turned to the people she had met along the way. She knew now how important it was to surround herself with those who lifted her up, not those who treated the Christian life like a competition, as if everyone were trying to be God's favorite. That was never His desire. He made each person exactly as He wanted them to be, with their own gifts, stories, and strengths. That is something to celebrate, not something to be ashamed of.

Yes, she could be bold and expressive, and at times she had let others make her feel as if these were negatives, as if she were somehow less than because she did not act like many other women. But as she looked back, she realized that the very qualities some tried to shame her for were the very ones God used to help her accomplish things that never would have been done had she been quiet or hesitant. Her boldness opened doors, her persistence carried her through storms, and her voice spoke truth when silence would have left wounds unhealed.

Of course, she was human, and she had not always used those qualities in the ways God intended. There were times when her expressiveness came out as frustration, when her boldness was more about proving herself than serving Him. Yet just as with everything else in her life, she was learning. She was learning how to temper strength with grace, how to let God shape her gifts so they could be used for His purpose instead of her pride.

What once felt like flaws now looked like tools in the hands of her Creator. She was not meant to be a copy of anyone else. God made her exactly as He wanted her to be, and that was something to celebrate, not something to hide in shame.

As she gazed out over the canyon, her mind filled with memories of blessings. Her children's laughter. Her mama's hand guiding her into church pews. The friends who carried her through storms. The kindness of strangers who helped her on the road. Each memory was a reminder that God had never left her, that His hope was always alive.

She smiled through her tears. "With You, Lord, there is always hope. To walk away from You is to walk away from hope itself. I do not want to forget that again."

CHAPTER ELEVEN: SEASONS OF PROMISE

Louella lingered in Big Bend for several days, soaking in the desert's quiet majesty. She hiked trails that wound through canyons, watched the sunrise spill over jagged cliffs, and sat at dusk as the stars returned in their endless sweep. Each moment felt like a gift, a reminder of God's hand in creation.

The desert taught her something she had not wanted to admit. For years she had filled her days with noise, work, worry, and endless tasks, forgetting the power of stillness. She realized she had not been getting into a quiet place with the Lord as often as she should. Without that time, her heart had sometimes been led astray, chasing approval or distraction instead of His presence.

Watching the sunrise over the canyon walls, Louella thought of how the rocks had been shaped by centuries of wind and water. They stood strong not because they resisted the elements, but because they yielded to them. In the same way, she knew her spirit was shaped when she yielded to God in prayer. Without that surrender, she was brittle, easily broken. With it, she was steady, even in storms.

At night, the stars stretched endlessly across the sky. Louella remembered how often she had rushed through life without looking up, without pausing to give God her full attention. The stars reminded her that His plans were vast, far beyond her own small worries. She whispered a prayer of repentance, asking the Lord to teach her to seek Him in silence, to listen before speaking, to rest before striving.

On her last morning there, she brewed coffee in Tess and sat at the little table with her laptop open. As she searched the internet for her next stop, a headline caught her eye: Wichita Mountains Wildlife Refuge. The photos showed rolling granite hills, wild bison grazing, and lakes tucked into valleys. Something about it stirred her spirit. She smiled, closed the lid, and whispered, "Alright, Lord. Let's see what You have waiting for me there."

It was nearly eight hours away. Louella packed up camp, secured Birdie's sunflower brooch on the dashboard, and pointed Tess north.

The day stretched long, the road winding through small towns and wide plains. With the hum of the tires beneath her, Louella found herself reflecting on her life. She had never regretted becoming a mother so early. It had been hard, many nights spent crying and praying out to God, wondering how she would make it through. As a single mother, there were times she thought she could not go on. Yet her children had kept her focused, kept her getting out of bed each morning when despair whispered otherwise.

Now, as the miles rolled by, her heart swelled with gratitude. All four of her children had grown into good, kind, capable adults. She was proud of them beyond words, and she credited God for every bit of it. He had carried her through the nights of doubt and the days of exhaustion, and He had blessed her children with strength and character.

But Louella also realized something new. Just because she no longer had children at home did not mean her purpose was over. Just because she was postmenopausal did not mean she was less than a complete woman. The words of Scripture echoed in her mind: *To everything there is a season.* She had given her all during her season of raising children, pouring herself out in love and sacrifice. And now, she owes it to herself, and to her children watching her, to give this season of life everything she had as well.

The freedom of the open road was not an escape, but a gift. It was a journey into a new season, a chance to live fully, to trust God with fresh purpose, and to show her children that life does not end when one chapter closes. It simply turns the page to another, equally important, equally blessed.

Journal Entry

The canyon reminded me that God is both artist and architect. Its walls bear His fingerprints, just as my life does. What I once called flaws are tools He is shaping for His purpose. I am unfinished, but not a mistake. Faith grows strongest in the quiet place, where His voice is clear and His presence is enough. As the canyon testifies to His power, I want my life to testify to His grace.

Me, Again

CHAPTER TWELVE: GOD'S GLORY

Louella had pulled into a quiet campground just outside the Wichita Mountains Wildlife Refuge the night before. The air was cooler here, carrying the scent of cedar and wild grass. She slept soundly, the hum of crickets and the distant call of owls lulling her into rest.

When morning came, sunlight filtered through the camper's curtains, painting the walls. Louella stretched, brewed a cup of coffee, and stepped outside. The campground was hushed, save for the rustle of leaves and the chatter of birds greeting the day. She breathed deeply, grateful for the stillness, grateful for the road that had carried her here.

Today was for exploring. She packed a small bag, tucked her journal inside, and whispered a prayer before locking Tess. "Lord, thank You for this new morning. Let me see Your beauty in every step."

The refuge stretched wide before her, a landscape of granite peaks, open prairie, and winding trails. Bison grazed in the distance, their massive forms moving slowly across the grasslands. A herd of elk lifted their heads as she passed, their antlers catching the light like crowns. Louella felt her heart swell. The beauty of God's creation was overwhelming, a reminder that His artistry was endless.

By midday, Louella found herself at a quiet lake tucked deep within the refuge. The water shimmered under the sun, rippling gently as the breeze moved across its surface. She settled onto a flat rock near the shore, unpacked the simple lunch she had brought: an apple, a sandwich, and a thermos of sweet tea. She let the stillness surround her.

As she ate, she watched the rhythm of nature unfold. A turtle eased slowly into the water, patient and unhurried. Dragonflies hovered above the reeds, their wings catching the light. Even the ripples on the lake seemed to move with purpose, never rushed, never forced. Louella realized that creation itself was teaching her patience. Nothing in nature demanded instant results. Growth, change, and beauty all took time.

Her thoughts drifted back to seasons in her own life when she had wanted things right away. Jobs she thought she needed, relationships she thought she could not live without, opportunities she had prayed for with urgency. At the time, she had been angry when doors closed and prayers seemed unanswered. Yet now, looking back, she could see how those very things would have harmed her, how they would have pulled her away from God's plan. What had felt like disappointment then had been protection all along.

She sighed, breaking off a piece of bread and tossing it toward the water where fish darted to the surface. "Lord, You knew better than I did. You always have."

Louella smiled softly, realizing that patience was not passive. It was trust. It was believing that God's timing was perfect, even when her own desires screamed for immediacy. She admitted to herself that she still failed at this from time to time. There were moments when she grew restless, when she wanted answers now, when she forgot that waiting was part of faith. But even in those failures, the truth remained: God's timing was always better than hers.

The lake reflected the sky like a mirror, and Louella felt her heart settle. She understood now that patience was not about denying desire but about surrendering it. It was about letting God shape her life in ways she could not yet see.

Journal Entry

Sitting by the lake today, I saw how nature teaches patience. Nothing blooms before its time. I remember the things I wanted so badly, the doors I begged You to open. At the time I was angry when they stayed shut, but now I see how those things would have hurt me. Thank You, Lord, for protecting me from what I thought I needed. Help me to trust Your timing, even when I fail, knowing that every season unfolds with purpose.

CHAPTER THIRTEEN: CALL OF THE COAST

Louella spent several more days exploring the refuge, letting its quiet beauty settle into her spirit. She wandered through meadows dotted with wildflowers, their colors bright against the rugged hills. One morning she climbed a trail that led to a fire tower, where the view stretched for miles in every direction, the granite peaks rising like ancient guardians of the land. In the evenings she sat quietly near a herd of longhorn cattle, marveling at their slow, deliberate movements and the way the setting sun painted their silhouettes in gold.

She found herself lingering by hidden springs and listening to the chorus of frogs at dusk, each sound reminding her that creation had its own rhythm and pace. At night, she spread a blanket beneath the stars, tracing constellations and whispering prayers of gratitude. The refuge taught her that life was not meant to be rushed. Every trail, every sunrise, every quiet encounter with wildlife reminded her that patience was part of God's design, and that His timing was always better than her own.

One morning, as she brewed coffee in Tess, her phone buzzed. Birdie's name lit up the screen. Louella smiled and answered.

"Where are you now?" Birdie asked, her voice bright with curiosity.

Louella laughed. "Still in Oklahoma. I have been at the Wichita Mountains Wildlife Refuge for a few days. It is beautiful out here."

"Well," Birdie said, "there is a festival down on the Mississippi coast next week. I thought of you the minute I heard about it. You should come."

Louella paused, then grinned. "I was just about to head back toward Florida anyway. That would be perfect."

Birdie gave her the details, describing the music, food, and coastal charm that awaited. Louella jotted it all down in her journal, already feeling the excitement of another destination pulling her forward.

Over the next few days, she drove south, taking her time. She stopped at roadside stands where farmers sold jars of honey and baskets of pecans. She lingered in small-town diners, savoring plates of fried catfish and cornbread while chatting with locals who treated her like family. Each stop reminded her of the richness of the journey, the way God's blessings often came in unexpected places.

By the time Louella reached the Mississippi coast, the air had changed. It was thick with salt and warmth, carrying the cry of gulls overhead and the steady rhythm of waves rolling against the shore. She parked Tess near the water and stepped out, letting the breeze lift her hair and the sound of the ocean wrap around her like a hymn.

The coastline stretched wide, dotted with fishing boats rocking gently in the harbors and piers lined with families casting lines into the surf. Children laughed as they chased one another along the sand, their voices mingling with the distant strum of a guitar from a beachside café. The scent of fried shrimp and hushpuppies drifted from a diner nearby, mingling with the briny tang of the sea.

Louella walked slowly along the boardwalk, taking it all in. Seashells crunched beneath her sandals, and pelicans swooped low over the water before diving for fish. She paused to watch the sun glint off the waves, each crest catching the light like a jewel. The coast was alive with movement and sound, yet it carried a peace that settled deep in her spirit.

She thought about Birdie's invitation to the festival and smiled. This place already felt like a celebration of life, of community, of God's creation. The ocean reminded her of His vastness, the endless horizon whispering that there was always more to discover, always more to trust.

That evening, Louella sat outside Tess with a plate of fresh seafood from a roadside shack, listening to the hum of cicadas and the crash of waves against the shore. She whispered a prayer of gratitude: "Lord, thank You for bringing me here. Thank You for the road, for the laughter, for the beauty of this coast. Help me to live this season fully, with joy and hope."

CHAPTER FOURTEEN: STEP OF FAITH

The Mississippi coast was alive with celebration. Music spilled from every corner of the festival grounds, a blend of blues and gospel that carried on the breeze and seemed to dance with the laughter of the crowd. The air was thick with the smell of fried shrimp, smoked ribs, and sweet kettle corn. Vendors lined the streets with colorful tents, selling handmade jewelry, painted seashells, and jars of jam that glistened in the sun.

Louella spotted Birdie near a booth where children were tossing rings onto bottles. Birdie waved, her smile as bright as the afternoon sky. "You made it!" she called, pulling Louella into a hug.

Together they wandered through the festival, playing games and sampling food from the stalls. Louella bit into a funnel cake dusted with powdered sugar, laughing as the sweetness clung to her fingers. Birdie insisted they try the roasted corn dripping with butter, and later they sat on a bench listening to a band play soulful tunes that made the crowd sway in rhythm.

As the sun began to dip low, they found a quieter spot near the edge of the festival grounds, where the sound of the music softened and the ocean breeze carried the scent of salt and fried fish. Louella leaned back against the bench and sighed.

"You know," she said, "I have always had people come up to me and share things, stories, burdens, encouragement. But this trip, starting with you, has been one moment after another like that. Everywhere I have gone, someone has crossed my path."

Birdie nodded, her eyes warm. "That is just how God works. Sometimes He is not mysterious at all. We are the ones who fail to recognize the obvious or reason it away. Every one of those people was placed in your path at the exact moment they needed to be. They were answers to the prayer you made before you started this journey."

Louella felt her chest swell with a mix of gratitude and awe, the kind that pressed tears to the surface before she could stop them. Her mind drifted back to the quiet morning in Florida when she had whispered a desperate prayer: "Lord, protect me on this journey. Help me find my meaning and purpose again. Guide me through the miles ahead and remind me that I am never truly alone." At the time, she had wondered if He had heard her at all. Yet now, sitting beside Birdie with the glow of festival lights shimmering against the night sky, she could see it clearly. Every encounter, every kindness, every unexpected moment along this journey had been His answer, unfolding piece by piece until she could no longer deny it.

She turned to Birdie, her voice trembling but steady. "You are right. He has been with me every step. I thought I was wandering, but all along He was leading. I just needed to stop questioning and open my eyes to see it."

Birdie squeezed her hand firmly, her smile gentle and knowing. "And you did, Louella. That is the beauty of it. Sometimes God's work is not hidden at all. It is right in front of us, waiting for us to recognize it."

Louella let the words sink in, the music from the festival drifting faintly in the background like a hymn. For the first time in a long time, she felt not only grateful but anchored, certain that her prayer had been answered in ways far greater than she had imagined.

As the festival lights flickered against the night sky and the music faded into the distance, Louella felt a quiet shift in her spirit. The joy of the coast had been a gift, the fellowship a reminder of God's provision, but now her heart stirred with a different kind of peace. She realized the journey had given her what she had prayed for: renewed purpose, fresh hope, and the assurance that God had been with her all along.

She looked out toward the waves, steady and unending, and whispered, "Thank You, Lord. I think I am ready now." The thought of home no longer felt heavy or uncertain. It felt like the next chapter, one she could step into with gratitude and faith.

CHAPTER FIFTEEN: COMPASS SET

The highway stretched wide before Louella as Tess carried her east toward Florida. Morning light spilled across the dashboard, glinting off Birdie's sunflower brooch, and Louella felt the steady rhythm of the tires beneath her like a hymn. The road itself seemed to sing of God's faithfulness.

She thought back to the prayer she had whispered before leaving home, asking the Lord to protect her and guide her toward meaning and purpose again. Now, with miles behind her, she could see how He had answered. Festivals, diners, quiet lakes, and strangers who became teachers. All of them had been threads in a tapestry only God could weave.

Louella realized her worth had never been lost. She had simply been looking in the wrong places. It was not in appearance, not in meeting expectations, not in chasing approval. Her value was in being the woman God created her to be, authentic and whole, living fully in His presence.

The seasons of her life had shifted, each carrying its own purpose. Motherhood had been one season, rediscovery another, and now she was stepping into a season of renewed faith. Scripture echoed in her heart: *To everything there is a season.* She had poured herself out in love for her children, and now she was learning to pour herself out in obedience to God's will.

A smile spread across her face as the road unfurled ahead. She wanted her journey to remind other women that true acceptance is not found in the world's standards but in God's truth. That their worth is steady, their purpose alive, and their hope anchored in Him.

As the Florida pines came into view, Louella whispered a prayer of gratitude. "Lord, thank You for every mile, every moment, every person You placed in my path. Thank You for reminding me that I am Yours. Help me to keep my eyes open, my heart steady, and my compass set on You."

The road home was not the end. It was the beginning of living with renewed purpose, carrying the lessons of the journey into every season yet to come.

CHAPTER SIXTEEN: FULL CIRCLE

The house was quiet when Louella returned, but the silence no longer felt heavy. It wrapped around her like a familiar embrace, steady and gentle. She set her bag down, brewed a cup of coffee, and sat at the kitchen table where countless meals had been shared and countless prayers had risen.

Her eyes drifted to the old Crock Pot on the counter, its chipped lid waiting. She smiled. It was more than a reminder of years gone by; it was a symbol of faithfulness, of a season poured out in love. She had given her all to raising her children, and now she was ready to give her all to this new season too.

She understood now that her worth was never lost. It was always anchored in God, waiting for her to remember. His presence had been steady in every mile, every storm, every kindness along the way.

She paused, listening to the hum of the refrigerator. Once it had sounded lonely. Tonight, it was grounding, a rhythm of home that reminded her of God's constancy.

Her prayer before the journey had been answered, not in one dramatic moment, but in countless small mercies: strangers who became teachers, laughter that lifted her spirit, storms that deepened her trust, and Birdie's wisdom that pointed her back to God. Each encounter had been His reminder that she was never alone.

Louella closed her journal and whispered, "Lord, let my compass always be You. Not the voices of others, not the world's expectations, but Your will alone."

The silence of the house was no longer empty. It was filled with miles traveled, lessons learned, and the assurance that every season of life carries purpose.

Final Road Trip Journal Entry

Tonight, as I sit in the quiet of my own home, I feel peace that only God can give. The silence is not emptiness; it is fullness, filled with His presence and the lessons of the road. This journey has shown me that deserts, storms, laughter, and mountaintops are all chapters in the same testimony. Each one was His reminder that I am not alone, that His love is unconditional, and that my life is part of His greater story.

This journey has ended, but it is not my end. New callings will rise, new ways to serve Him will unfold. My compass is set on God, and wherever He leads, I will follow with gratitude and trust. Tonight, I rest, knowing that my story is His story, and that every season ahead will be for His glory.

ABOUT THE AUTHOR

Adrienne Forehand grew up in Holmes County, Florida and now resides in Tallahassee. A proud mother of four adult children and grandmother of four, she is embracing her lifelong dream of writing fiction that inspires reflection and hope. Adrienne's stories are heartfelt and relatable, offering encouragement without ignoring life's challenges. Her greatest joy is knowing that even one reader might find comfort or strength in her words. She gives all glory to God, praising Him for His grace and mercy, and writes with the desire to uplift, connect, and remind others that faith and resilience can light the way forward.

Made in the USA
Coppell, TX
07 December 2025

64986733R00025